The Little Red Hen

Written by Nikki Gamble

Illustrated by Scott Nash

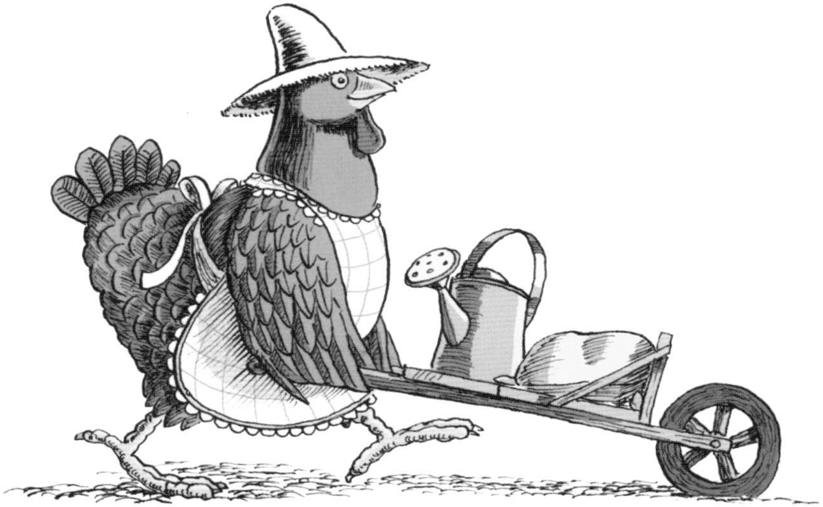

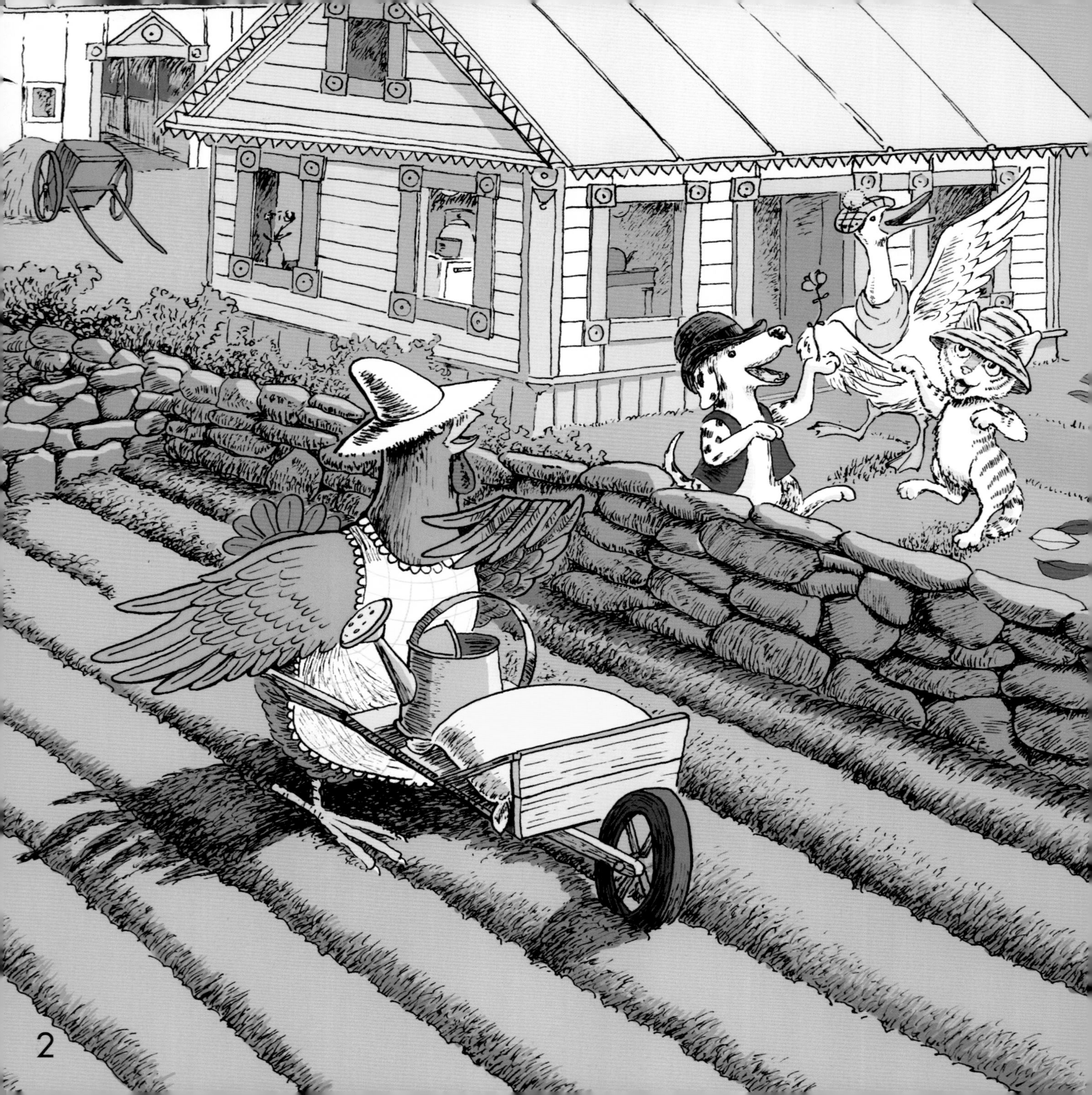

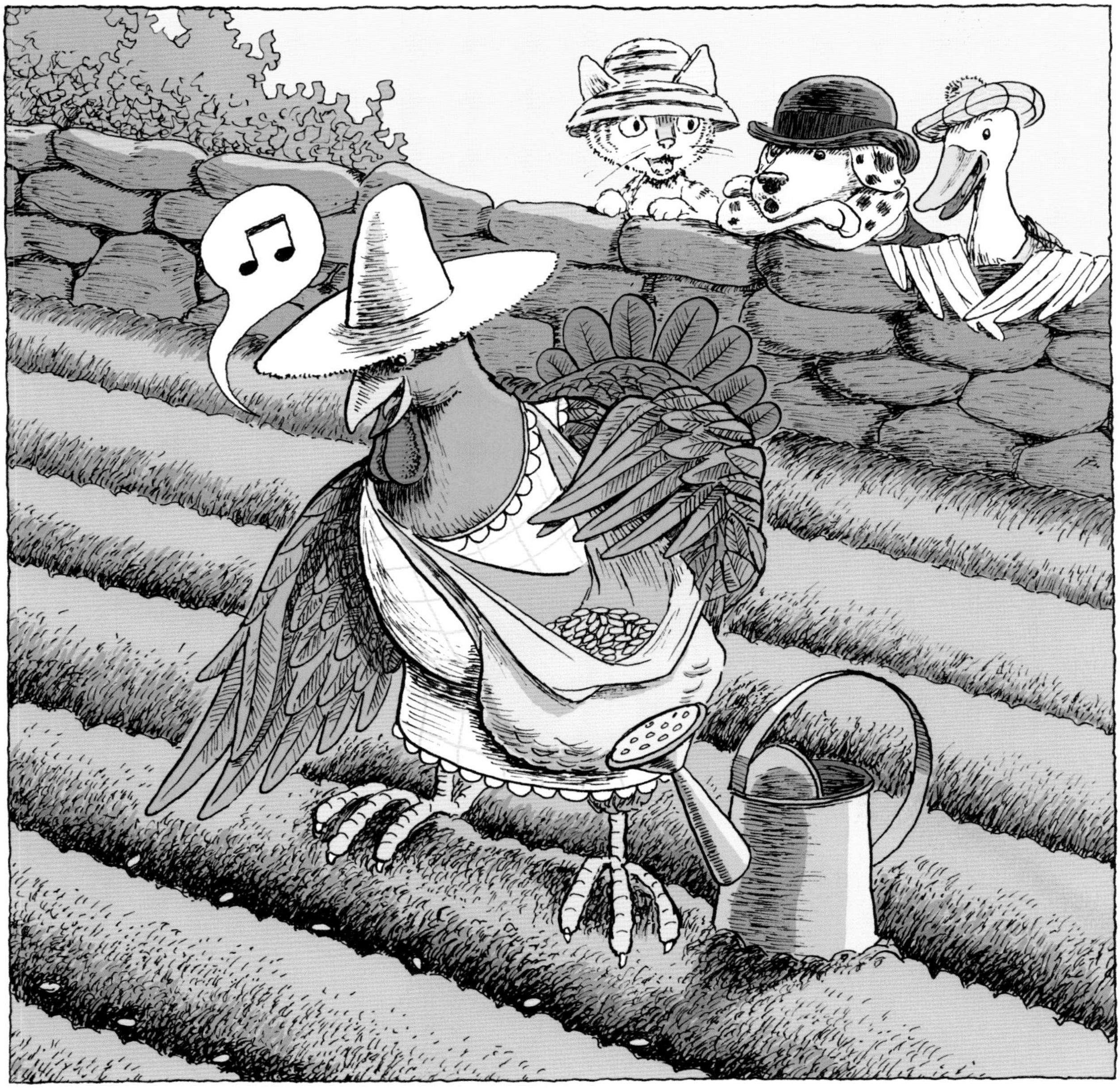

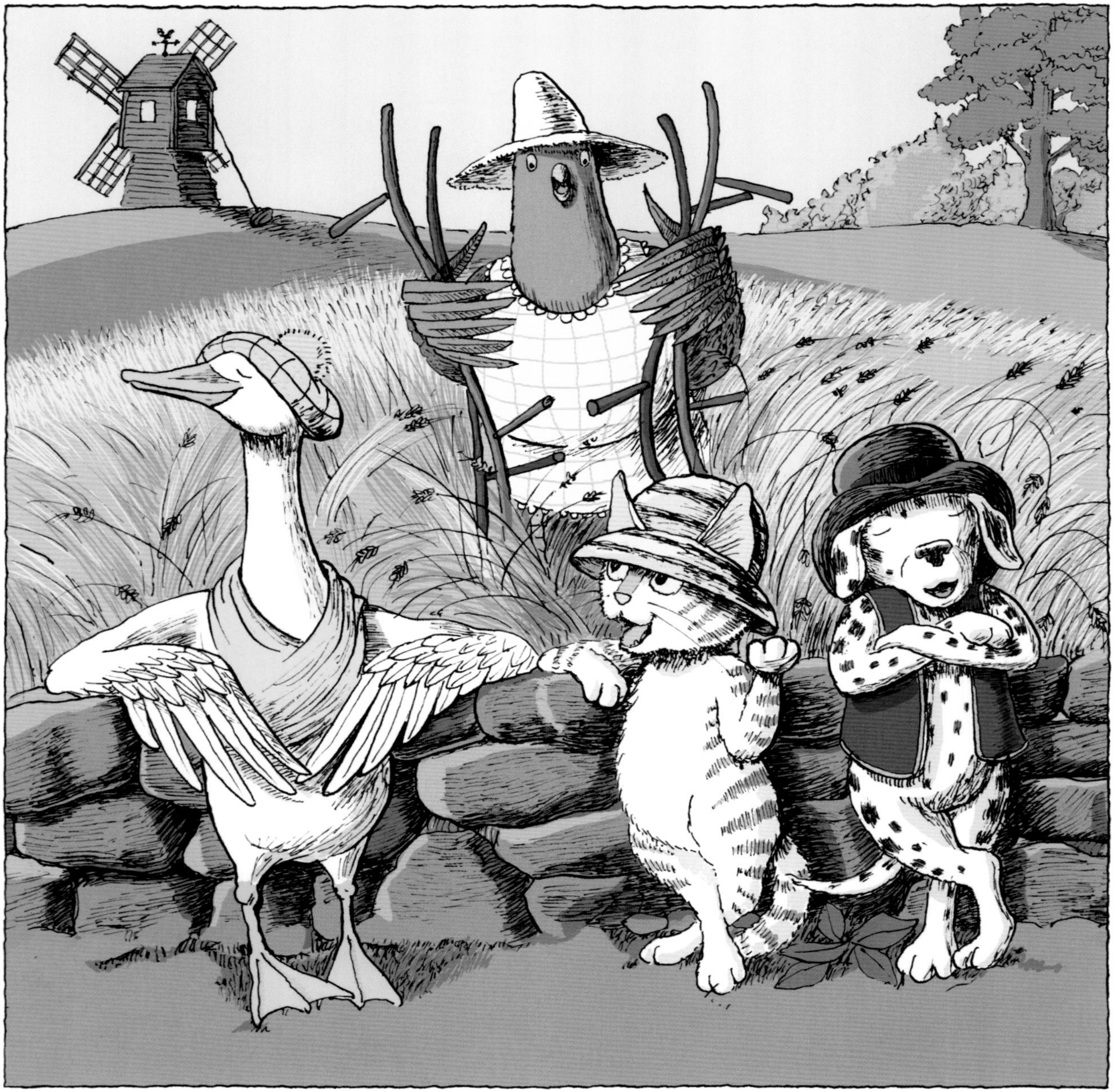

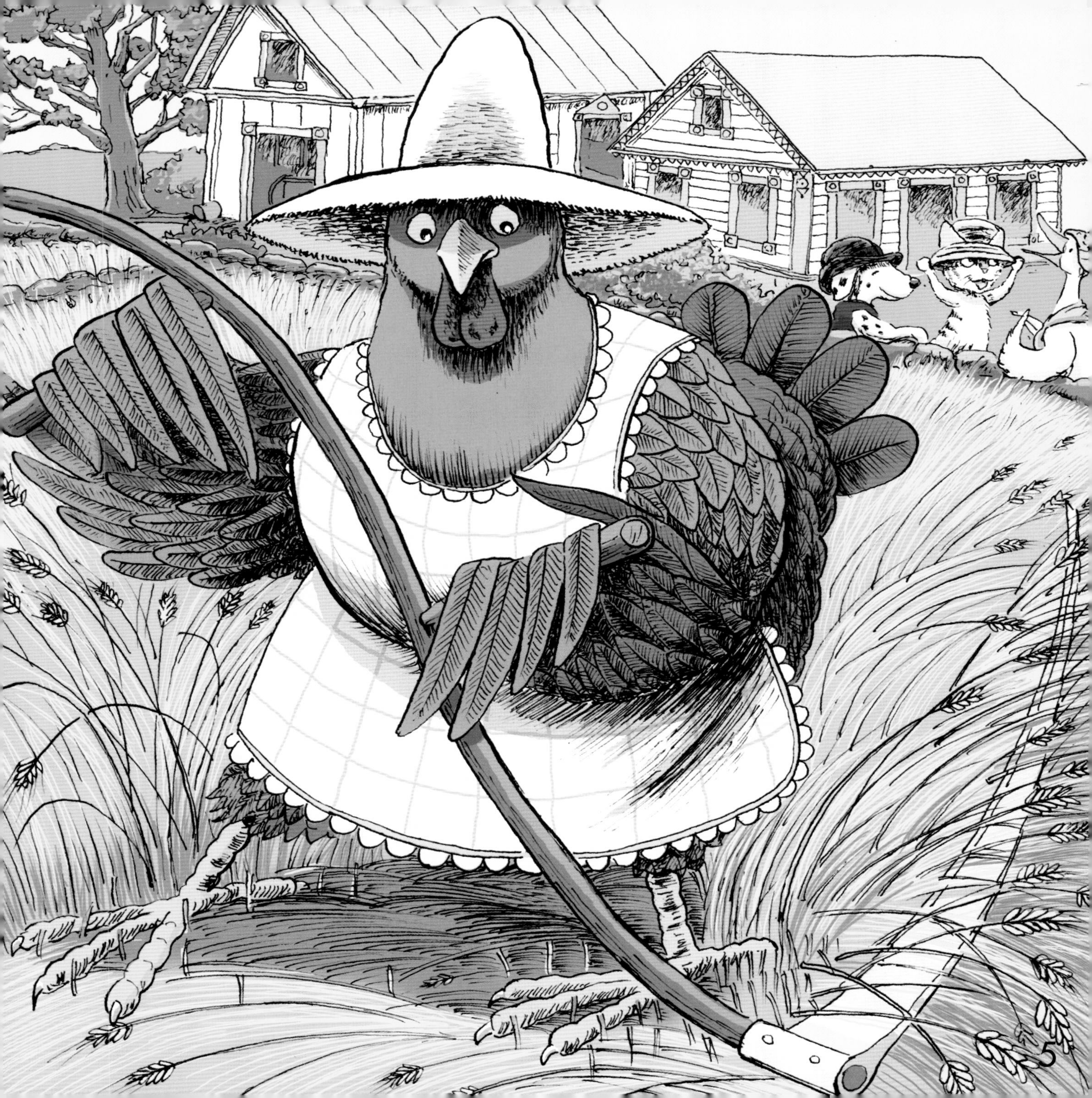

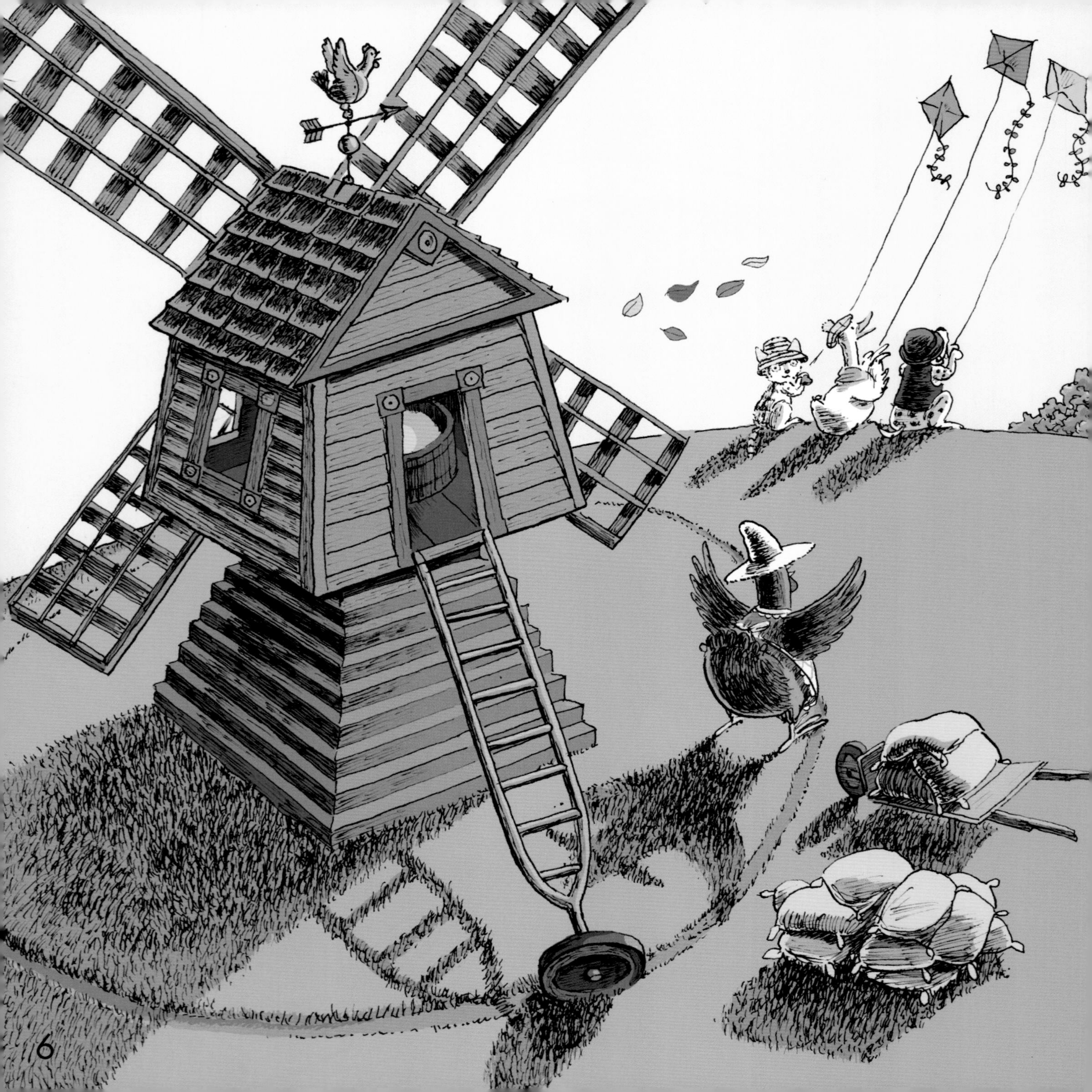

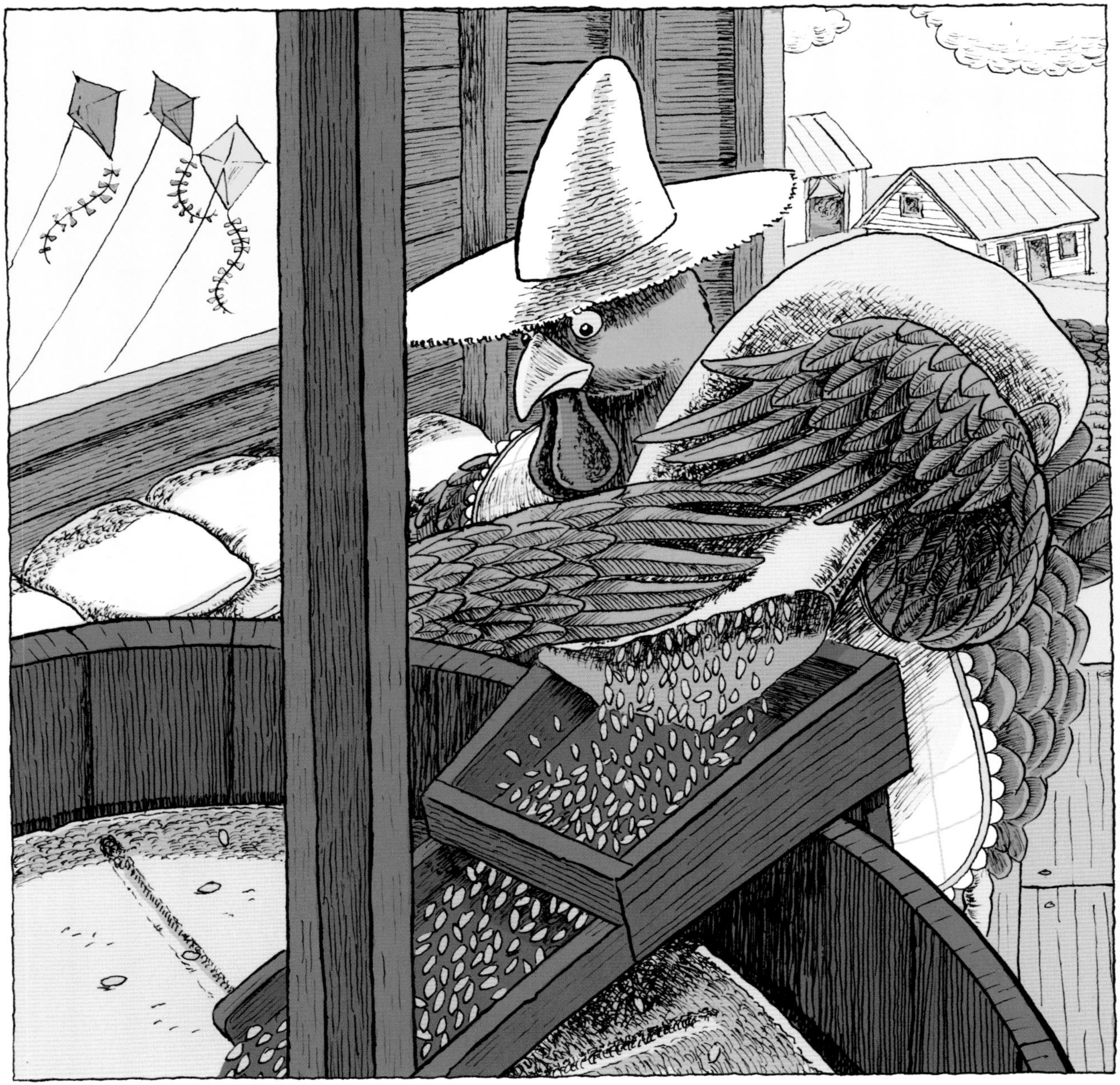

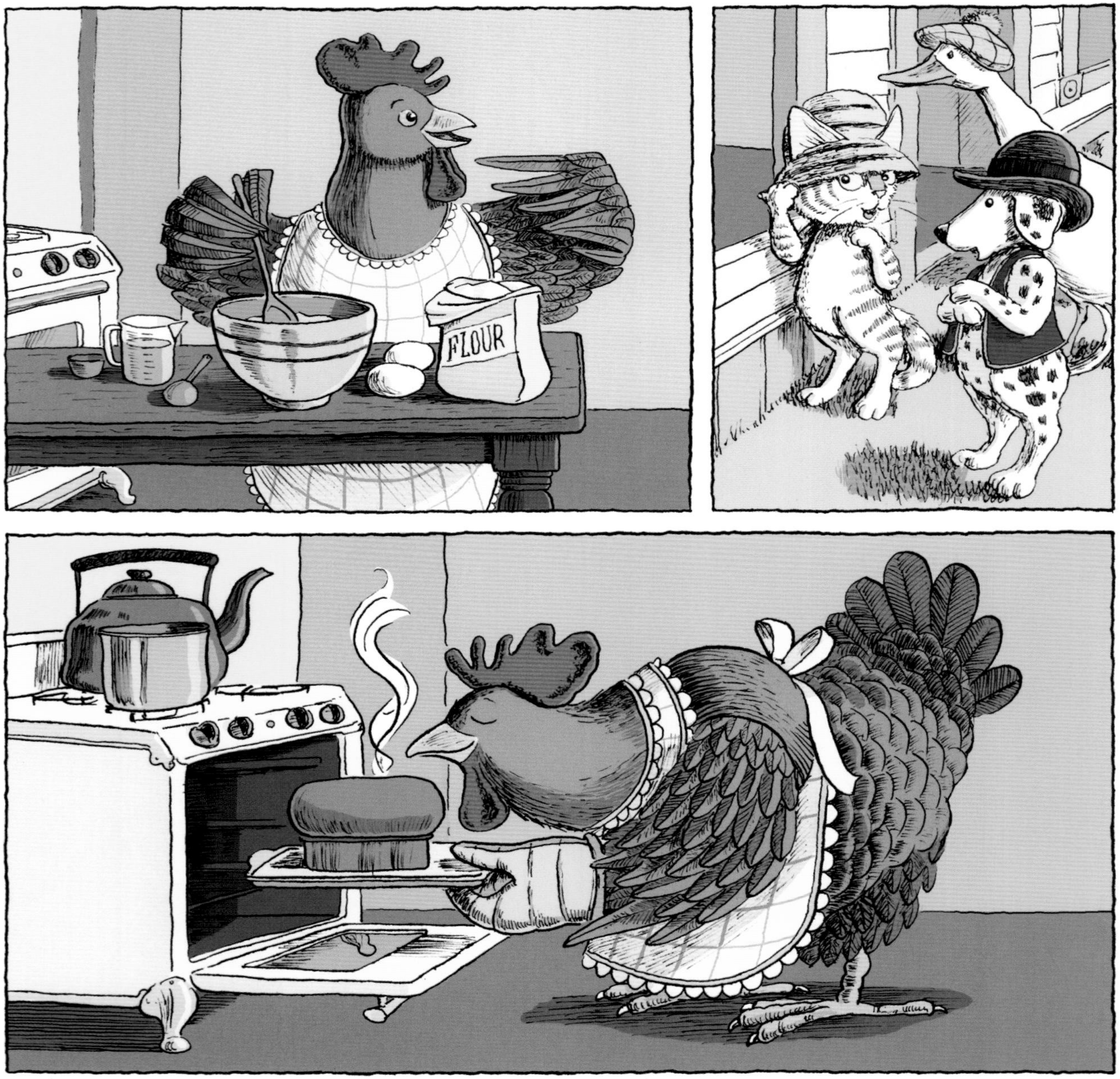
FLOUR

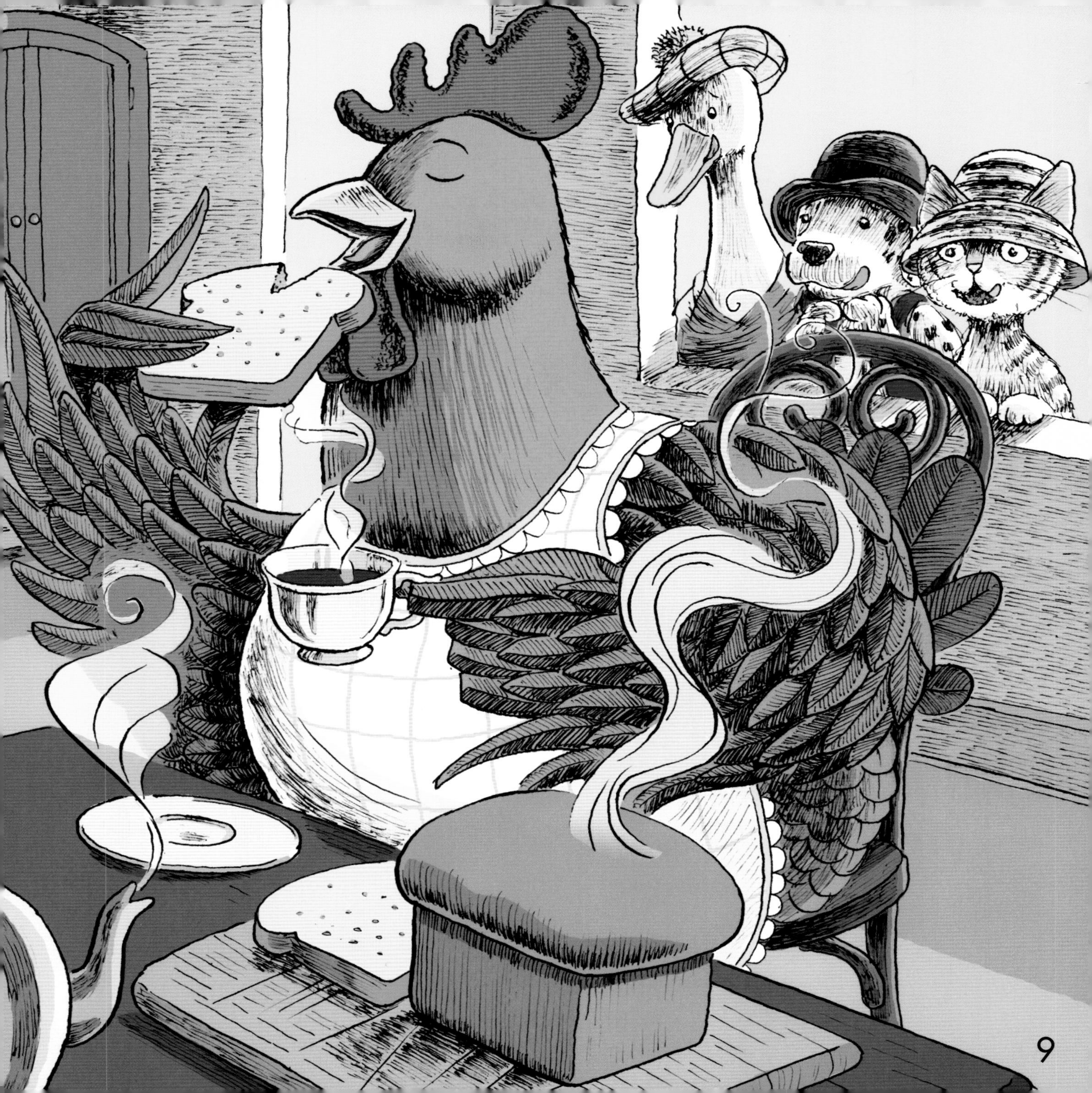

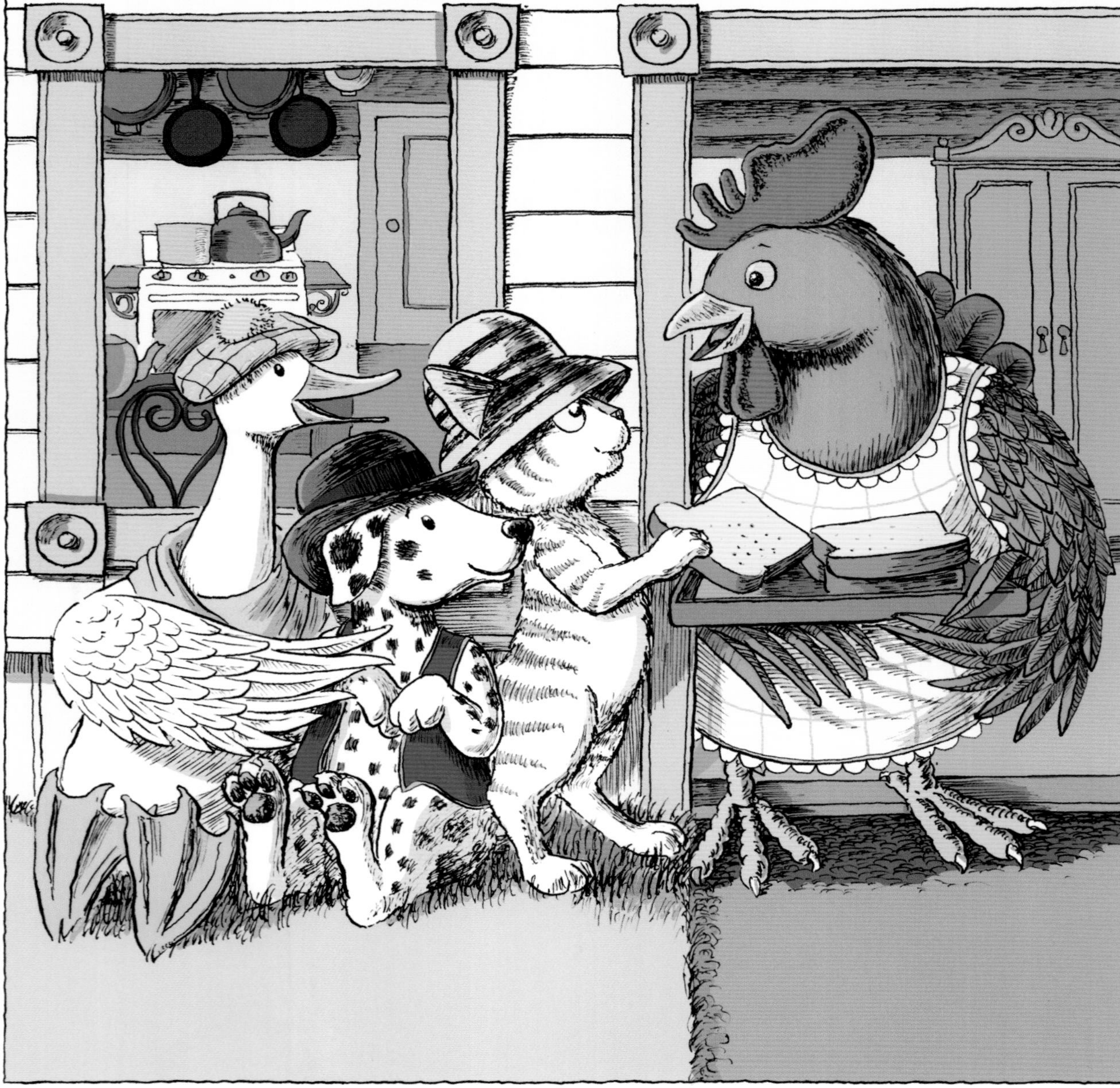

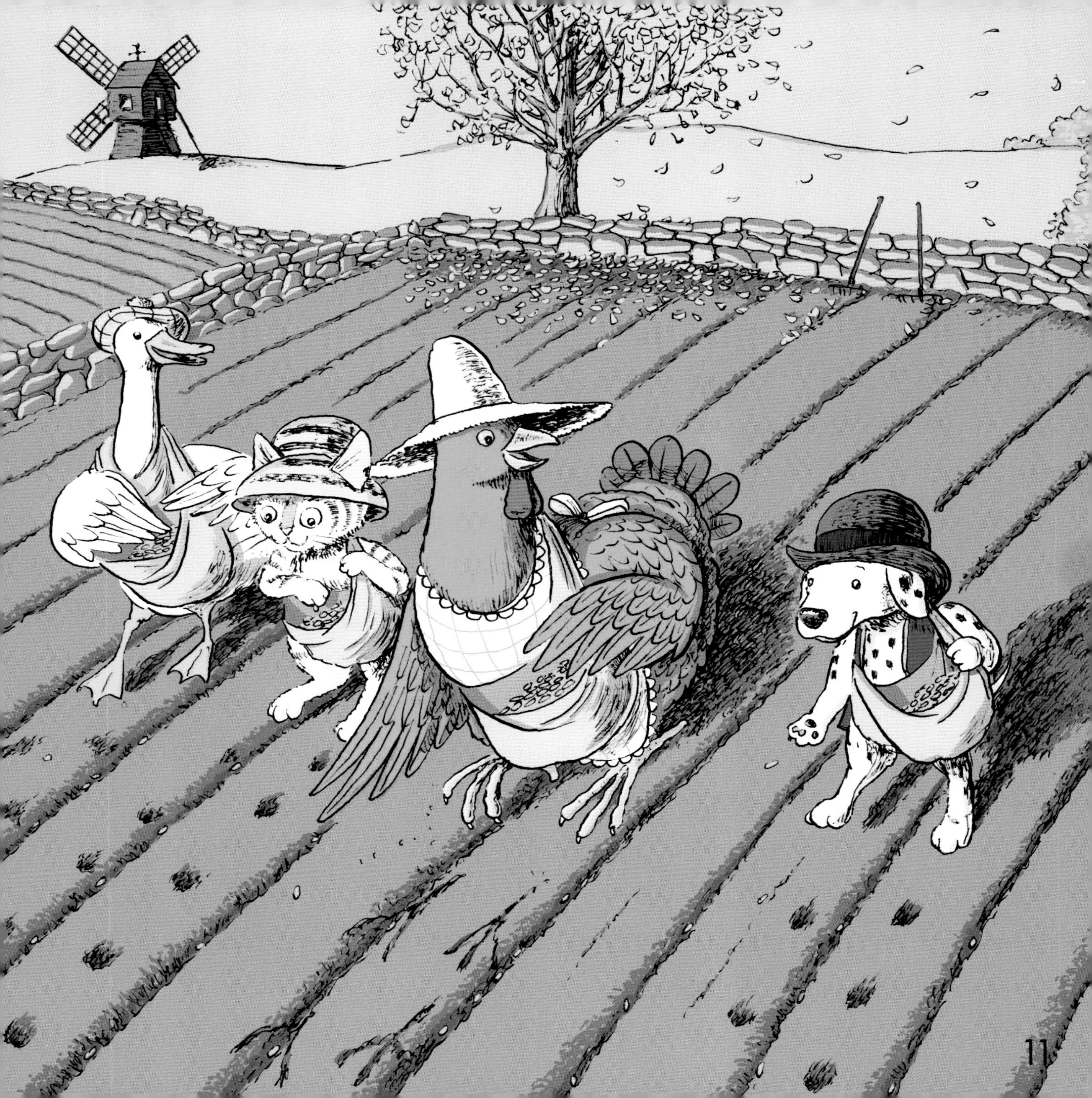

Retell the story

Once upon a time...

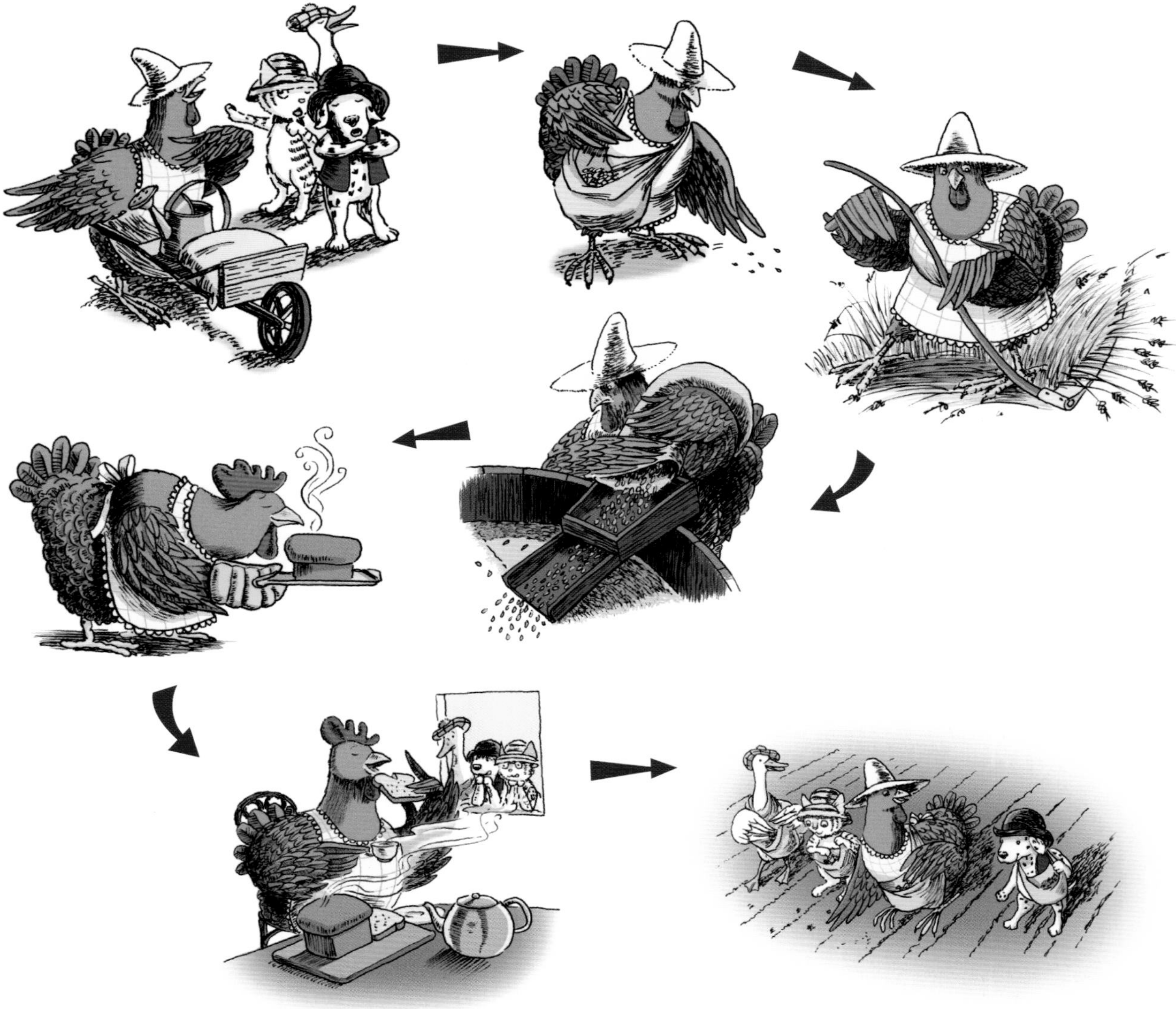

The end.